The Sandman

E.T.A. Hoffmann

ISBN-13: 978-1537604848

Table of Contents

Nathaniel to Lothaire

Certainly you must all be uneasy that I have not written for so long—so very long. My mother, am sure, is angry, and Clara will believe that I am passing my time in dissipation, entirely forgetful of her fair, angelic image that is so deeply imprinted on my heart. Such, however, is not the case. Daily and hourly I think of you all; and the dear form of my lovely Clara passes before me in my dreams, smiling upon me with her bright eyes as she did when I was among you. But how can I write to you in the distracted mood which has been disturbing my every thought! A horrible thing has crossed my path. Dark forebodings of a cruel, threatening fate tower over me like dark clouds, which no friendly sunbeam can penetrate. I will now tell you what has occurred. I must do so—that I plainly see—the mere thought of it sets me laughing like a madman. Ah, my dear Lothaire, how shall I begin ? How shall I make you in any way realize that what happened to me a few days ago can really have had such a fatal effect on my life? If you were here you could see for yourself; but, as it is, you will certainly take me for a crazy fellow who sees ghosts. To be brief, this horrible occurrence, the painful impression of which I am in vain endeavoring to throw off, is nothing more than this—that some days ago, namely on the 30th of October at twelve o'clock noon, a barometer-dealer came into my room and offered me his wares. I bought nothing, and threatened to throw him downstairs, upon which he took himself off of his own accord.

Only circumstances of the most peculiar kind, you will suspect, and exerting the greatest influence over my life, can have given any import to this occurrence. Moreover, the person of that unlucky dealer must have had an evil effect upon me. So it was, indeed. I must use every endeavor to collect myself, and patiently and quietly tell you so much of my early youth as will bring the picture plainly and clearly before your eyes. As I am about to begin, I fancy that I hear you laughing, and Clara exclaiming, 'Childish stories indeed!' Laugh at me, I beg of you, laugh with all your heart. But, oh God! my hair stands on end, and it is in mad despair that I seem to be inviting your laughter, as Franz Moor did Daniel's in Schiller's play. But to my story.

Excepting at dinner-time I and my brothers and sisters used to see my father very little during the day. He was, perhaps, busily engaged at his ordinary profession. After supper, which was served according to the old custom at seven o'clock, we all went with my mother into my father's study, and seated ourselves at the round table, where he would smoke and drink his large glass of beer. Often he told us wonderful stories, and grew so warm over them that his pipe continually went out. Whereupon I had to light it again with a burning spill, which I thought great sport. Often, too, he would give us picture-books, and sit in his armchair, silent and thoughtful, puffing out such thick clouds of smoke that we all seemed to be swimming in the clouds. On such evenings as these my mother was very melancholy, and immediately the clock struck nine she would say: 'Now, children, to bed—to bed! The Sandman's coming, I can see.' And indeed on each occasion I used to hear something with a heavy, slow step come thudding up the stairs. That I thought must be the Sandman.

Once when the dull noise of footsteps was particularly terrifying I asked my mother as she bore us away: 'Mamma, who is this naughty Sandman, who always drives us away from Papa? What does he look like?'

'There is no Sandman, dear child,' replied my mother. 'When I say the Sandman's coming, I only mean that you're sleepy and can't keep your eyes open—just as if sane had been sprinkled into them.'

This answer of my mother's did not satisfy me—nay, the thought soon ripened in my childish mind the she only denied the Sandman's existence to prevent our being terrified of him. Certainly I always heard him coming up the stairs. Most curious to know more of this Sandman and his particular connection with children, I at last asked the old woman who looked after my youngest sister what sort of man he was.

'Eh, Natty,' said she, 'don't you know that yet? He is a wicked man, who comes to children when they won't go to bed, and throws a handful of sand into their eyes, so that they start out bleeding from their heads. He puts their eyes in a bag and carries them to the crescent moon to feed his own children, who sit in the nest up there. They have crooked beaks like owls so that they can pick up the eyes of naughty human children.'

A most frightful picture of the cruel Sandman became impressed upon my mind; so that when in the evening I heard the noise on the stairs I trembled with agony and alarm, and my mother could get nothing out of me but the cry, 'The Sandman, the Sandman!' stuttered forth through my tears. I then ran into the bedroom, where the frightful apparition of the Sandman terrified me during the whole night.

I had already grown old enough to realize that the nurse's tale about him and the nest of children in the crescent moon could not be quite true, but nevertheless this Sandman remained a fearful spectre, and I was seized with the utmost horror when I heard him once, not only come up the stairs, but violently force my father's door open and go in. Sometimes he stayed away for a long period, but after that his visits came in close succession. This lasted for years, but I could not accustom myself to the terrible goblin; the image of the dreadful Sandman did not become any fainter. His intercourse with my father began more and more to occupy my fancy. Yet an unconquerable fear prevented me from asking my father about it. But if I, I myself, could penetrate the mystery and behold the wondrous Sandman—that was the wish which grew upon me with the years. The Sandman had introduced me to thoughts of the marvels and wonders which so readily gain a hold on a child's mind. I enjoyed nothing better than reading or hearing horrible stories of goblins, witches, pigmies, etc.; but most horrible of all was the Sandman, whom I was always drawing with chalk or charcoal on the tables, cupboards and walls, in the oddest and most frightful shapes.

When I was ten years old my mother removed me from the night nursery into a little chamber situated in a corridor near my father's room. Still, as before, we were obliged to make a speedy departure on the stroke of nine, as soon as the unknown step sounded on the stair. From my little chamber I could hear how he entered my father's room, and then it was that I seemed to detect a thin vapor with a singular odor spreading through the house. Stronger and stronger, with my curiosity, grew my resolution somehow to make the Sandman's acquaintance. Often I sneaked from my room to the corridor when my mother had passed, but never could I discover anything; for the Sandman had always gone in at the door when I reached the place where I might have seen him. At last, driven by an irresistible impulse, I resolved to hide myself in my father's room and await his appearance there.

From my father's silence and my mother's melancholy face I perceived one evening that the Sandman was coming. I, therefore, feigned great weariness, left the room before nine o'clock, and hid myself in a corner close to the door. The house-door groaned and the heavy, slow, creaking step came up the passage and towards the stairs. My mother passed me with the rest of the children. Softly, very softly, I opened the door of my father's room. He was sitting, as usual, stiff end silent, with his back to the door. He did not perceive me, and I swiftly darted into the room and behind the curtain which covered an open cupboard close to the door, in which my father's clothes were hanging. The steps sounded nearer and nearer—there was a strange coughing and scraping and murmuring without. My heart trembled with anxious expectation. A sharp step close, very close, to the door—the quick snap of the latch, and the door opened with a rattling noise. Screwing up my courage to the uttermost, I cautiously peeped out. The Sandman was standing before my father in the middle of the room, the light of the candles shone full upon his face. The Sandman, the fearful Sandman, was the old advocate Coppelius, who had often dined with us.

But the most hideous form could not have inspired me with deeper horror than this very Coppelius. Imagine a large broad-shouldered man, with a head disproportionately big, a face the color of yellow ochre, a pair of bushy grey eyebrows, from beneath which a pair of green cat's eyes sparkled with the most penetrating luster, and with a large nose curved over his upper lip. His wry mouth was often twisted into a malicious laugh, when a couple of dark red spots appeared upon his cheeks, and a strange hissing sound was heard through his gritted teeth. Coppelius always appeared in an ashen-gray coat, cut in old fashioned style, with waistcoat and breeches of the same color, while his stockings were black, and his shoes adorned with agate buckles.

His little peruke scarcely reached farther than the crown of his head, his curls stood high above his large red ears, and a broad hair-bag projected stiffly from his neck, so that the silver clasp which fastened his folded cravat might be plainly seen. His whole figure was hideous and repulsive, but most disgusting to us children were his coarse brown hairy fists. Indeed we did not like to eat anything he had touched with them. This he had noticed, and it was his delight, under some pretext or other, to touch a piece of cake or some nice fruit, that our kind mother might quietly have put on our plates, just for the pleasure of seeing us turn away with tears in our eyes, in disgust and abhorrence, no longer able to enjoy the treat intended for us. He acted in the same manner on holidays, when my father gave us a little glass of sweet wine. Then would he swiftly put his hand over it, or perhaps even raise the glass to his blue lips, laughing most devilishly, and we could only express our indignation by silent sobs. He always called us the little beasts; we dared not utter a sound when he was present, end we heartily cursed the ugly, unkind man who deliberately marred our slightest pleasures. My mother seemed to hate the repulsive Coppelius as much as we did, since as soon as he showed himself her liveliness, her open and cheerful nature, were changed for a gloomy solemnity. My father behaved towards him as though he were a superior being, whose bad manners were to be tolerated and who was to be kept in good humor at any cost. He need only give the slightest hint, and favorite dishes were cooked, the choicest wines served.

When I now saw this Coppelius, the frightful and terrific thought took possession of my soul, that indeed no one but he could be the Sandman. But the Sandman was no longer the bogy of a nurse's tale, who provided the owl's nest in the crescent moon with children's eyes. No, he was a hideous, spectral monster, who brought with him grief, misery and destruction—temporal and eternal—wherever he appeared.

I was riveted to the spot, as if enchanted. At the risk of being discovered and, as I plainly foresaw, of being severely punished, I remained with my head peeping through the curtain. My father received Coppelius with solemnity.

'Now to our work!' cried the latter in a harsh, grating voice, as he flung off his coat.

My father silently and gloomily drew off his dressing gown, and both attired themselves in long black frocks. Whence they took these I did not see. My father opened the door of what I had always thought to be a cupboard. But I now saw that it was no cupboard, but rather a black cavity in which there was a little fireplace. Coppelius went to it, and a blue flame began to crackle up on the hearth. All sorts of strange utensils lay around. Heavens! As my old father stooped down to the fire, he looked quite another man. Some convulsive pain seemed to have distorted his mild features into a repulsive, diabolical countenance. He looked like Coppelius, whom I saw brandishing red-hot tongs, which he used to take glowing masses out of the thick smoke; which objects he afterwards hammered. I seemed to catch a glimpse of human faces lying around without any eyes—but with deep holes instead.

'Eyes here' eyes!' roared Coppelius tonelessly. Overcome by the wildest terror, I shrieked out and fell from my hiding place upon the floor. Coppelius seized me and, baring his teeth, bleated out, 'Ah—little wretch—little wretch!' Then he dragged me up and flung me on the hearth, where the fire began to singe my hair. 'Now we have eyes enough—a pretty pair of child's eyes,' he whispered, and, taking some red-hot grains out of the flames with his bare hands, he was about to sprinkle them in my eyes.

My father upon this raised his hands in supplication, crying: 'Master, master, leave my Nathaniel his eyes!'

Whereupon Coppelius answered with a shrill laugh: 'Well, let the lad have his eyes and do his share of the world's crying, but we will examine the mechanism of his hands and feet.'

And then he seized me so roughly that my joints cracked, and screwed off my hands and feet, afterwards putting them back again, one after the other. 'There's something wrong here,' he mumbled. 'But now it's as good as ever. The old man has caught the idea!' hissed and lisped Coppelius. But all around me became black, a sudden cramp darted through my bones and nerves—and I lost consciousness. A gentle warm breath passed over my face; I woke as from the sleep of death. My mother had been stooping over me.

'Is the Sandman still there?' I stammered.

'No, no, my dear child, he has gone away long ago—he won't hurt you!' said my mother, kissing her darling, as he regained his senses.

Why should I weary you, my dear Lothaire, with diffuse details, when I have so much more to tell ? Suffice it to say that I had been discovered eavesdropping and ill-used by Coppelius. Agony and terror had brought on delirium and fever, from which I lay sick for several weeks.

'Is the Sandman still there?' That was my first sensible word and the sign of my amendment—my recovery. I have only to tell you now of this most frightful moment in all my youth, and you will be convinced that it is no fault of my eyes that everything seems colorless to me. You will, indeed, know that a dark fatality has hung over my life a gloomy veil of clouds, which I shall perhaps only tear away in death.

Coppelius was no more to be seen; it was said he had left the town.

About a year might have elapsed, and we were sitting, as of old, at the round table. My father was very cheerful, and was entertaining us with stories about his travels in his youth; when, as the clock struck nine, we heard the house-door groan on its hinges, and slow steps, heavy as lead, creaked through the passage and up the stairs.

'That is Coppelius,' said my mother, turning pale.

'Yes!—that is Coppelius" repeated my father in a faint, broken voice. The tears started to my mother's eyes.

'But father—father!' she cried, 'must it be so?'

'He is coming for the last time, I promise you,' was the answer. 'Only go now, go with the children—go—go to bed. Good night!'

I felt as if I were turned to cold, heavy stone—my breath stopped. My mother caught me by the arm as I stood immovable. 'Come, come, Nathaniel!' I allowed myself to be led, and entered my chamber! 'Be quiet—be quiet—go to bed—go to sleep!' cried my mother after me; but tormented by restlessness and an inward anguish perfectly indescribable, I could not close my eyes.

The hateful, abominable Coppelius stood before me with fiery eyes, and laughed maliciously at me. It was in vain that I endeavored to get rid of his image. About midnight there was a frightful noise, like the firing of a gun. The whole house resounded. There was a rattling and rustling by my door, and the house door was closed with a violent bang.

'That is Coppelius !' I cried, springing out of bed in terror.

Then there was a shriek, as of acute, inconsolable grief. I darted into my father's room; the door was open, a suffocating smoke rolled towards me, and the servant girl cried: 'Ah, my master, my master!' On the floor of the smoking hearth lay my father dead, with his face burned, blackened and hideously distorted—my sisters were shrieking and moaning around him—and my mother had fainted.

'Coppelius!—cursed devil! You have slain my father!' I cried, and lost my senses.

When, two days afterwards, my father was laid in his coffin, his features were again as mild and gentle as they had been in his life. My soul was comforted by the thought that his compact with the satanic Coppelius could not have plunged him into eternal perdition.

The explosion had awakened the neighbors, the occurrence had become common talk, and had reached the ears of the magistracy, who wished to make Coppelius answerable. He had, however, vanished from the spot, without leaving a trace.

If I tell you, my dear friend, that the barometer-dealer was the accursed Coppelius himself, you will not blame me for regarding so unpropitious a phenomenon as the omen of some dire calamity. He was dressed differently, but the figure and features of Coppelius are too deeply imprinted in my mind for an error in this respect to be possible. Besides, Coppelius has not even altered his name. He describes himself, I am told, as a Piedmontese optician, and calls himself Giuseppe Coppola.

I am determined to deal with him, and to avenge my father's death, be the issue what it may.

Tell my mother nothing of the hideous monster's appearance. Remember me to my dear sweet Clara, to whom I will write in a calmer mood. Farewell.

Clara to Nathaniel

It is true that you have not written to me for a long time; but, nevertheless, I believe that I am still in your mind and thoughts. For assuredly you were thinking of me most intently when, designing to send your last letter to my brother Lothaire, you directed it to me instead of to him. I joyfully opened the letter, and did not perceive my error till I came to the words: 'Ah, my dear Lothaire.'

NO, by rights I should have read no farther, but should have handed over the letter to my brother. Although you have often, in your childish teasing mood, charged me with having such a quiet, womanish, steady disposition, that, even if the house were about to fall in, I should smooth down a wrong fold in the window curtain in a most ladylike manner before I ran away, I can hardly tell you how your letter shocked me. I could scarcely breathe-----the light danced before my eyes.

Ah, my dear Nathaniel, how could such a horrible thing have crossed your path ? To be parted from you, never to see you again—the thought darted through my breast like a burning dagger. I read on and on. Your description of the repulsive Coppelius is terrifying. I learned for the first time the violent manner of your good old father's death. My brother Lothaire, to whom I surrendered the letter, sought to calm me, but in vain. The fatal barometer dealer, Giuseppe Coppola, followed me at every step; and I am almost ashamed to confess that he disturbed my healthy and usually peaceful sleep with all sorts of horrible visions. Yet soon even the next day—I was quite changed again. Do not be offended, dearest one, if Lothaire tells you that in spite of your strange fears that Coppelius will in some manner injure you, I am in the same cheerful and unworried mood as ever.

I must honestly confess that, in my opinion, all the terrible things of which you speak occurred merely in your own mind, and had little to do with the actual external world. Old Coppelius may have been repulsive enough, but his hatred of children was what really caused the abhorrence you children felt towards him.

In your childish mind the frightful Sandman in the nurse's tale was naturally associated with old Coppelius. Why, even if you had not believed in the Sandman, Coppelius would still have seemed to you a monster, especially dangerous to children. The awful business which he carried on at night with your father was no more than this: that they were making alchemical experiments in secret, which much distressed your mother since, besides a great deal of money being wasted, your father's mind was filled with a fallacious desire after higher wisdom, and so alienated from his family—as they say is always the case with such experimentalists. Your father, no doubt, occasioned his own death, by some act of carelessness of which Coppelius was completely guiltless. Let me tell you that I yesterday asked our neighbor, the apothecary, whether such a sudden and fatal explosion was possible in these chemical experiments?

'Certainly,' he replied and, after his fashion, told me at great length and very circumstantially how such an event might take place, uttering a number of strange-sounding names which I am unable to recollect. Now, I know you will be angry with your Clara; you will say that her cold nature is impervious to any ray of the mysterious, which often embraces man with invisible arms; that she only sees the variegated surface of the world, and is as delighted as a silly child at some glittering golden fruit, which contains within it a deadly poison.

Ah ! my dear Nathaniel! Can you not then believe that even in open, cheerful, careless minds may dwell the suspicion of some dread power which endeavors to destroy us in our own selves ? Forgive me, if I, a silly girl, presume in any manner to present to you my thoughts on such an internal struggle. I shall not find the right words, of course, and you will laugh at me, not because my thoughts are foolish, but because I express them so clumsily.

If there is a dark and hostile power, laying its treacherous toils within us, by which it holds us fast and draws us along the path of peril and destruction, which we should not otherwise have trod; if, I say there is such a power, it must form itself inside us and out of ourselves, indeed; it must become identical with ourselves. For it is only in this condition that we can believe in it, and grant it the room which it requires to accomplish its secret work. Now, if we have a mind which is sufficiently firm, sufficiently strengthened by the joy of life, always to recognize this strange enemy as such, and calmly to follow the path of our own inclination and calling, then the dark power will fail in its attempt to gain a form that shall be a reflection of ourselves. Lothaire adds that if we have willingly yielded ourselves up to the dark powers, they are known often to impress upon our minds any strange, unfamiliar shape which the external world has thrown in our way; so that we ourselves kindle the spirit, which we in our strange delusion believe to be speaking to us. It is the phantom of our own selves, the close relationship with which, and its deep operation on our mind, casts us into hell or transports us into heaven.

You see, dear Nathaniel, how freely Lothaire and I are giving our opinion on the subject of the dark powers; which subject, to judge by my difficulties in writing down. its most important features, appears to be a complicated one. Lothaire's last words I do not quite comprehend. I can only suspect what he means, and yet I feel as if it were all very true. Get the gruesome advocate Coppelius, and the barometer-dealer, Giuseppe Coppola, quite out of your head, I beg of you. Be convinced that these strange fears have no power over you, and that it is only a belief in their hostile influence that can make them hostile in reality. If the great disturbance in your mind did not speak from every line of your letter, if your situation did not give me the deepest pain, I could joke about the Sandman-Advocate and the barometer dealer Coppelius. Cheer up, I have determined to play the part of your guardian-spirit. If the ugly Coppelius takes it into his head to annoy you in your dreams, I'll scare him away with loud peals of laughter. I am not a bit afraid of him nor of his disgusting hands; he shall neither spoil my sweetmeats as an Advocate, nor my eyes as a Sandman. Ever yours, my dear Nathaniel.

Nathaniel to Lothaire

I am very sorry that in consequence of the error occasioned by my distracted state of mind, Clara broke open the letter intended for you, and read it. She has written me a very profound philosophical epistle, in which she proves, at great length, that Coppelius and Coppola only exist in my own mind, and are phantoms of myself, which will be dissipated directly I recognize them as such. Indeed, it is quite incredible that the mind which so often peers out of those bright, smiling, childish eyes with all the charm of a dream, could make such intelligent professorial definitions. She cites you—you, it seems have been talking about me. I suppose you read her logical lectures, so that she may learn to separate and sift all matters acutely. No more of that, please. Besides, it is quite certain that the barometer-dealer, Giuseppe Coppola, is not the advocate Coppelius. I attend the lectures of the professor of physics, who has lately arrived. His name is the same as that of the famous natural philosopher Spalanzani, and he is of Italian origin. He has known Coppola for years and, moreover, it is clear from his accent that he is really a Piedmontese. Coppelius was a German, but I think no honest one. Calmed I am not, and though you and Clara may consider me a gloomy visionary, I cannot get rid of the impression which the accursed face of Coppelius makes upon me. I am glad that Coppola has left the town—so Spalanzani says.

This professor is a strange fellow—a little round man with high cheek-bones, a sharp nose, pouting lips and little, piercing eyes. Yet you will get a better notion of him than from this description, if you look at the portrait of Cagliostro, drawn by Chodowiecki in one of the Berlin annuals; Spalanzani looks like that exactly. I lately went up his stairs, and perceived that the curtain, which was generally drawn completely over a glass door, left a little opening on one side. I know not what curiosity impelled me to look through. A very tall and slender lady, extremely well-proportioned and most splendidly attired, sat in the room by a little table on which she had laid her arms, her hands being folded together. She sat opposite the door, so that I could see the whole of her angelic countenance. She did not appear to see me, and indeed there was something fixed about her eyes as if, I might almost say, she had no power of sight. It seemed to me that she was sleeping with her eyes open. I felt very uncomfortable, and therefore I slunk away into the lecture-room close at hand.

Afterwards I learned that the form I had seen was that of Spalanzani's daughter Olympia, whom he keeps confined in a very strange and barbarous manner, so that no one can approach her. After all, there may be something the matter with her; she is half-witted perhaps, or something of the kind. But why should I write you all this? I could have conveyed it better and more circumstantially by word of mouth. For I shall see you in a fortnight. I must again behold my dear, sweet angelic Clara. My evil mood will then be dispersed, though I must confess that it has been struggling for mastery over me ever since her sensible but vexing letter. Therefore I do not write to her today. A thousand greetings, etc.

Nothing more strange and chimerical can be imagined than the fate of my poor friend, the young student Nathaniel, which I, gracious reader, have undertaken to tell you. Have you ever known something that has completely filled your heart, thoughts and senses, to the exclusion of every other object? There was a burning fermentation within you; your blood seethed like a molten glow through your veins, sending a higher color to your cheeks. Your glance was strange, as if you were seeking in empty space forms invisible to all other eyes, and your speech flowed away into dark sighs. Then your friends asked you: 'What is it, my dear sir?' 'What is the matter?' And you wanted to draw the picture in your mind in all its glowing tints, in all its light and shade, and labored hard to find words only to begin. You thought that you should crowd together in the very first sentence all those wonderful, exalted, horrible, comical, frightful events, so as to strike every hearer at once as with an electric shock. But every word, every thing that takes the form of speech, appeared to you colorless, cold and dead. You hunt and hunt, and stutter and stammer, and your friends' sober questions blow like icy wind upon your internal fire until it is almost out. Whereas if, like a bold painter, you had first drawn an outline of the internal picture with a few daring strokes, you might with small trouble have laid on the colors brighter and brighter, and the living throng of varied shapes would have borne your friends away with it. Then they would have seen themselves, like you, in the picture that your mind had bodied forth. Now I must confess to you, kind reader, that no one has really asked me for the history of the young Nathaniel, but you know well enough that I belong to the queer race of authors who, if they have anything in their minds such as I have just described, feel as if everyone who comes near them, and the whole world besides, is insistently demanding: 'What is it then—tell it, my dear friend?'

Thus was I forcibly compelled to tell you of the momentous life of Nathaniel. The marvelous singularity of the story filled my entire soul, but for that very reason and because, my dear reader, I had to make you equally inclined to accept the uncanny, which is no small matter, I was puzzled how to begin Nathaniel's story in a manner as inspiring, original and striking as possible. 'Once upon a time,' the beautiful beginning of every tale, was too tame. 'In the little provincial town of S____ lived'—was somewhat better, as it at least prepared for the climax. Or should I dart at once, medias in res, with '"Go to the devil," cried the student Nathaniel with rage and horror in his wild looks, when the barometer-dealer, Giuseppe Coppola . . .?'—I had indeed already written this down, when I fancied that I could detect something ludicrous in the wild looks of the student Nathaniel, whereas the story is not comical at all. No form of language suggested itself to my mind which seemed to reflect ever in the slightest degree the coloring of the internal picture. I resolved that I would not begin it at all.

So take, gentle reader, the three letters. which friend Lothaire was good enough to give me, as the sketch of the picture which I shall endeavor to color more and more brightly as I proceed with my narrative. Perhaps, like a good portrait-painter, I may succeed in catching the outline in this way, so that you will realize it is a likeness even without knowing the original, and feel as if you had often seen the person with your own corporeal eyes. Perhaps, dear reader, you will then believe that nothing is stranger and madder than actual life; which the poet can only catch in the form of a dull reflection in a dimly polished mirror.

To give you all the information that you will require for a start, we must supplement these letters with the news that shortly after the death of Nathaniel's father, Clara and Lothaire, the children of a distant relative, who had likewise died and left them orphans, were taken by Nathaniel's mother into her own home.

Clara and Nathaniel formed a strong attachment for each other; and no one in the world having any objection to make, they were betrothed when Nathaniel left the place to pursue his studies in G____ . And there he is, according to his last letter, attending the lectures of the celebrated professor of physics, Spalanzani.

Now, I could proceed in my story with confidence, but at this moment Clara's picture stands so plainly before me that I cannot turn away; as indeed was always the case when she gazed at me with one of her lovely smiles. Clara could not by any means be reckoned beautiful, that was the opinion of all who are by their calling competent judges of beauty. Architects, nevertheless, praised the exact symmetry of her frame, and painters considered her neck, shoulders and bosom almost too chastely formed; but then they all fell in love with her wondrous hair and coloring, comparing her to the Magdalen in Battoni's picture at Dresden. One of them, a most fantastical and singular fellow, compared Clara's eyes to a lake by Ruysdael, in which the pure azure of a cloudless sky, the wood and flowery field, the whole cheerful life of the rich landscape are reflected. Poets and composers went still further. 'What is a lake what is a mirror!' said they. 'Can we look upon the girl without wondrous, heavenly music flowing towards us from her glances, to penetrate our inmost soul so that all there is awakened and stirred? If we don't sing well then, there is not much in us, as we shall learn from the delicate smile which plays on Clara's lips, when we presume to pipe up before her with something intended to pass for a song, although it is only a confused jumble of notes.'

So it was. Clara had the vivid fancy of a cheerful, unembarrassed child; a deep, tender, feminine disposition; an acute, clever understanding. Misty dreamers had not a chance with her; since, though she did not talk—talking would have been altogether repugnant to her silent nature—her bright glance and her firm ironical smile would say to them: 'Good friends, how can you imagine that I shall take your fleeting shadowy images for real shapes imbued with life and motion?' On this account Clara was censured by many as cold, unfeeling and prosaic; while others, who understood life to its clear depths, greatly loved the feeling, acute, childlike girl; but none so much as Nathaniel, whose perception in art and science was clear and strong. Clara was attached to her lover with all her heart, and when he parted from her the first cloud passed over her life. With what delight, therefore, did she rush into his arms when, as he had promised in his last letter to Lothaire, he actually returned to his native town and entered his mother's room! Nathaniel's expectations were completely fulfilled; for directly he saw Clara he thought neither of the Advocate Coppelius nor of her 'sensible' letter. All gloomy forebodings had gone.

However, Nathaniel was quite right, when he wrote to his friend Lothaire that the form of the repulsive barometer-dealer, Coppola, had had a most evil effect on his life. All felt, even in the first days, that Nathaniel had undergone a complete change in his whole being. He sank into a gloomy reverie, and behaved in a strange manner that had never been known in him before. Everything, his whole life, had become to him a dream and a foreboding, and he was always saying that man, although he might think himself free, only served for the cruel sport of dark powers These he said it was vain to resist; man must patiently re-sign himself to his fate. He even went so far as to say that it is foolish to think that we do anything in art and science according to our own independent will; for the inspiration which alone en-ables us to produce anything does not proceed from within our-selves, but is the effect of a higher principle without.

To the clear-headed Clara this mysticism was in the highest degree repugnant, but contradiction appeared to be useless. Only when Nathaniel proved that Coppelius was the evil principle, which had seized him at the moment when he was listening be-hind the curtain, and that this repugnant principle would in some horrible manner disturb the happiness of their life, Clara grew very serious, and said: 'Yes, Nathaniel, you are right. Coppelius is an evil, hostile principle; he can produce terrible effects, like a diabolical power that has come visibly into life; but only if you will not banish him from your mind and thoughts. So long as you believe in him, he really exists and exerts his influence; his power lies only in your belief.'

Quite indignant that Clara did not admit the demon's exist-ence outside his own mind, Nathaniel would then come out with all the mystical doctrine of devils and powers of evil. But Clara would break off peevishly by introducing some indifferent mat-ter, to the no small annoyance of Nathaniel. He thought that such deep secrets were closed to cold, unreceptive minds, without being clearly aware that he was counting Clara among these subordinate natures; and therefore he constantly endeavored to initiate her into the mysteries. In the morning, when Clara was getting breakfast ready, he stood by her, reading out of all sorts of mystical books till she cried: 'But dear Nathaniel, suppose I blame you as the evil principle that has a hostile effect upon my coffee? For if, to please you, I drop everything and look in your eyes while you read, my coffee will overflow into the fire, and none of you will get any breakfast.'

Nathaniel closed the book at once and hurried indignantly to his chamber. Once he had a remarkable forte for graceful, lively tales, which he wrote down, and to which Clara listened with the greatest delight; now his creations were gloomy, incomprehensible and formless, so that although, out of compassion, Clara did not say so, he plainly felt how little she was interested. Nothing was more unbearable to Clara than tediousness; her looks and words expressed mental drowsiness which she could not overcome. Nathaniel's productions were, indeed, very tedious. His indignation at Clara's cold, prosaic disposition constantly increased; and Clara could not overcome her dislike of Nathaniel's dark, gloomy, boring mysticism, so that they became mentally more and more estranged without either of them perceiving it. The shape of the ugly Coppelius, as Nathaniel himself was forced to confess, was growing dimmer in his fancy, and it often cost him some pains to draw him with sufficient color in his stories, where he figured as the dread bogy of ill omen.

It occurred to him, however, in the end to make his gloomy foreboding, that Coppelius would destroy his happiness, the subject of a poem. He represented himself and Clara as united by true love, but occasionally threatened by a black hand, which appeared to dart into their lives, to snatch away some new joy just as it was born. Finally, as they were standing at the altar, the hideous Coppelius appeared and touched Clara's lovely eyes. They flashed into Nathaniel's heart, like bleeding sparks, scorching and burning, as Coppelius caught him, and flung him into a flaming, fiery circle, which flew round with the swiftness of a storm, carrying him along with it, amid its roaring. The roar is like that of the hurricane, when it fiercely lashes the foaming waves, which rise up, like black giants with white heads, for the furious combat. But through the wild tumult he hears Clara's voice: 'Can't you see me then? Coppelius has deceived you. Those, indeed, were not my eyes which so burned in your breast—they were glowing drops of your own heart's blood. I have my eyes still—only look at them!' Nathaniel reflects: 'That is Clara, and I am hers for ever!' Then it seems to him as though this thought has forcibly entered the fiery circle, which stands still, while the noise dully ceases in the dark abyss. Nathaniel looks into Clara's eyes, but it is death that looks kindly upon him from her eyes

While Nathaniel composed this poem, he was very calm and collected; he polished and improved every line, and having subjected himself to the fetters of metre, he did not rest till all was correct and melodious. When at last he had finished and read the poem aloud to himself, a wild horror seized him. 'Whose horrible voice is that?' he cried out. Soon, however, the whole appeared to him a very successful work, and he felt that it must rouse Clara's cold temperament, although he did not clearly consider why Clara was to be excited, nor what purpose it would serve to torment her with frightful pictures threatening a horrible fate, destructive to their love. Both of them—that is to say, Nathaniel and Clara—were sitting in his mother's little garden, Clara very cheerful, because Nathaniel had not teased her with his dreams and his forebodings during the three days in which he had been writing his poem.

He was even talking cheerfully, as in the old days, about pleasant matters, which caused Clara to remark: 'Now for the first time I have you again! Don't you see that we have driven the ugly Coppelius away?'

Not till then did it strike Nathaniel that he had in his pocket the poem, which he had intended to read. He at once drew the sheets out and began, while Clara, expecting something tedious as usual, resigned herself and began quietly to knit. But as the dark cloud rose ever blacker and blacker, she let the stocking fall and looked him full in the face. He was carried irresistibly along by his poem, an internal fire deeply reddened his cheeks, tears flowed from his eyes.

At last, when he had concluded, he groaned in a state of utter exhaustion and, catching Clara's hand, sighed forth, as if melted into the most inconsolable grief: 'Oh Clara!—Clara!' Clara pressed him gently to her bosom, and said softly, but very solemnly and sincerely: 'Nathaniel, dearest Nathaniel, do throw that mad, senseless, insane stuff into the fire!'

Upon this Nathaniel sprang up enraged and, thrusting Clara from him, cried: 'Oh, inanimate, accursed automaton!'

With which he ran off; Clara, deeply offended, shed bitter tears, and sobbed aloud: 'Ah, he has never loved me, for he does not understand me.'

Lothaire entered the arbor; Clara was obliged to tell him all that had occurred. He loved his sister with all his soul, and every word of her complaint fell like a spark of fire into his heart, so that the indignation which he had long harbored against the visionary Nathaniel now broke out into the wildest rage. He ran to Nathaniel and reproached him for his senseless conduce towards his beloved sister in hard words, to which the infuriated Nathaniel retorted in the same style. The appellation of 'fantastical, mad fool,' was answered by that of 'miserable commonplace fellow.' A duel was inevitable. They agreed on the following morning, according to the local student custom, to fight with sharp rapiers on the far side of the garden. Silently and gloomily they slunk about. Clara had overheard the violent dispute and, seeing the fencing-master bring the rapiers at dawn, guessed what was to occur.

Having reached the place of combat, Lothaire and Nathaniel had in gloomy silence flung off their coats, and with the lust of battle in their flaming eyes were about to fall upon one another, when Clara rushed through the garden door, crying aloud between her sobs: 'You wild cruel men! Strike me down before you attack each other. For how can I live on if my lover murders my brother, or my brother murders my lover.'

Lothaire lowered his weapon, and looked in silence on the ground; but in Nathaniel's heart, amid the most poignant sorrow, there revived all his love for the beautiful Clara, which he had felt in the prime of his happy youth. The weapon fell from his hand, he threw himself at Clara's feet. 'Can you ever forgive me, my only—my beloved Clara? Can you forgive me, my dear brother, Lothaire?'

Lothaire was touched by the deep contrition of his friend; all three embraced in reconciliation amid a thousand tears, and vowed eternal love and fidelity.

Nathaniel felt as though a heavy and oppressive burden had been rolled away, as though by resisting the dark power that held him fast he had saved his whole being, which had been threatened with annihilation. Three happy days he passed with his dear friends, and then went to G___ , where he intended to stay a year, and then to return to his native town for ever.

All that referred to Coppelius was kept a secret from his mother. For it was well known that she could not think of him without terror since she, as well as Nathaniel, held him guilty of causing her husband's death.

How surprised was Nathaniel when, proceeding to his lodging, he saw that the whole house was burned down, and that only the bare walls stood up amid the ashes. However, although fire had broken out in the laboratory of the apothecary who lived on the ground-floor, and had therefore consumed the house from top to bottom, some bold active friends had succeeded in entering Nathaniel's room in the upper story in time to save his books, manuscripts and instruments. They carried all safe and sound into another house, where they took a room, to which Nathaniel moved at once. He did not think it at all remarkable that he now lodged opposite to Professor Spalanzani; neither did it appear singular when he perceived that his window looked straight into the room where Olympia often sat alone, so that he could plainly recognize her figure, although the features of her face were indistinct and confused. At last it struck him that Olympia often remained for hours in that attitude in which he had once seen her through the glass door, sitting at a little table without any occupation, and that she was plainly enough looking over at him with an unvarying gaze. He was forced to confess that he had never seen a more lovely form but, with Clara in his heart, the stiff Olympia was perfectly indifferent to him. Occasionally, to be sure, he gave a transient look over his textbook at the beautiful statue, but that was all.

He was just writing to Clara, when he heard a light tap at the door; it stopped as he answered, and the repulsive face of Coppola peeped in. Nathaniel's heart trembled within him, but remembering what Spalanzani had told him about his compatriot Coppola, and also the firm promise he had made to Clara with respect to the Sandman Coppelius, he felt ashamed of his childish fear and, collecting himself with all his might, said as softly and civilly as possible: 'I do not want a barometer, my good friend; pray go.'

Upon this, Coppola advanced a good way into the room, his wide mouth distorted into a hideous laugh, and his little eyes darting fire from beneath their long grey lashes: 'Eh, eh—no barometer—no barometer?' he said in a hoarse voice, 'I have pretty eyes too—pretty eyes!'

'Madman!' cried Nathaniel in horror. 'How can you have eyes? Eyes?'

But Coppola had already put his barometer aside and plunged his hand into his wide coat-pocket, whence he drew lorgnettes and spectacles, which he placed upon the table.

'There—there—spectacles on the nose, those are my eyes— pretty eyes!' he gabbled, drawing out more and more spectacles, until the whole table began to glisten and sparkle in the most extraordinary manner.

A thousand eyes stared and quivered, their gaze fixed upon Nathaniel; yet he could not look away from the table, where Coppola kept laying down still more and more spectacles, and all those flaming eyes leapt in wilder and wilder confusion, shooting their blood red light into Nathaniel's heart.

At last, overwhelmed with horror, he shrieked out: 'Stop, stop, you terrify me!' and seized Coppola by the arm, as he searched his pockets to bring out still more spectacles, although the whole table was already covered.

Coppola gently extricated himself with a hoarse repulsive laugh; and with the words: 'Ah, nothing for you—but here are pretty glasses!' collected all the spectacles, packed them away, and from the breast-pocket of his coat drew forth a number of telescopes large and small. As soon as the spectacles were removed Nathaniel felt quite easy and, thinking of Clara, perceived that the hideous phantom was but the creature of his own mind, that this Coppola was an honest optician and could not possibly be the accursed double of Coppelius. Moreover, in all the glasses which Coppola now placed on the table, there was nothing remarkable, or at least nothing so uncanny as in the spectacles; and to set matters right Nathaniel resolved to make a purchase. He took up a little, very neatly constructed pocket telescope, and looked through the window to try it. Never in his life had he met a glass which brought objects so clearly and sharply before his eyes. Involuntarily he looked into Spalanzani's room; Olympia was sitting as usual before the little table, with her arms laid upon it, and her hands folded.

For the first time he could see the wondrous beauty in the shape of her face; only her eyes seemed to him singularly still and dead. Nevertheless, as he looked more keenly through the glass, it seemed to him as if moist moonbeams were rising in Olympia's eyes. It was as if the power of seeing were being kindled for the first time; her glances flashed with constantly increasing life. As if spellbound, Nathaniel reclined against the window, meditating on the charming Olympia. A humming and scraping aroused him as if from a dream.

Coppola was standing behind him: 'Tre zecchini—three ducats!' He had quite forgotten the optician, and quickly paid him what he asked. 'Is it not so ? A pretty glass—a pretty glass ?' asked Coppola, in his hoarse, repulsive voice, and with his malicious smile.

'Yes—yes,' replied Nathaniel peevishly; 'Good-bye, friend.'

Coppola left the room, but not without casting many strange glances at Nathaniel. He heard him laugh loudly on the stairs.

'Ah,' thought Nathaniel, 'he is laughing at me because, no doubt, I have paid him too much for this little glass.'

While he softly uttered these words, it seemed as if a deep and lugubrious sigh were sounding fearfully through the room; and his breath was stopped by inward anguish. He perceived, however, that it was himself that had sighed.

'Clara is right,' he said to himself, 'in taking me for a senseless dreamer, but it is pure madness—nay, more than madness, that the stupid thought of having paid Coppola too much for the glass still pains me so strangely. I cannot see the cause.'

He now sat down to finish his letter to Clara; but a glance through the window assured him that Olympia was still sitting there, and he instantly sprang up, as if impelled by an irresistible power, seized Coppola's glass, and could not tear himself away from the seductive sight of Olympia till his friend and brother Sigismund called him to go to Professor Spalanzani's lecture. The curtain was drawn close before the fatal room, and he could see Olympia no longer, nor could he upon the next day or the next, although he scarcely ever left his window and constantly looked through Coppola's glass. On the third day the windows were completely covered. In utter despair, filled with a longing and a burning desire, he ran out of the town-gate. Olympia's form floated before him in the air, stepped forth from the bushes, and peeped at him with large beaming eyes from the clear brook. Clara's image had completely vanished from his mind; he thought of nothing but Olympia, and complained aloud in a murmuring voice: 'Ah, noble, sublime star of my love, have you only risen upon me to vanish immediately, and leave me in dark hopeless night?'

As he returned to his lodging, however, he perceived a great bustle in Spalanzani's house. The doors were wide open, all sorts of utensils were being carried in, the windows of the first floor were being taken out, maid-servants were going about sweeping and dusting with great hairbrooms, and carpenters and upholsterers were knocking and hammering within. Nathaniel remained standing in the street in a state of perfect wonder, when Sigismund came up to him laughing, and said: 'Now, what do you say to our old Spalanzani?'

Nathaniel assured him that he could say nothing because he knew nothing about the professor, but on the contrary perceived with astonishment the mad proceedings in a house otherwise so quiet and gloomy. He then learnt from Sigismund that Spalanzani intended to give a grand party on the following day—a concert and ball—and that half the university was invited. It was generally reported that Spalanzani, who had so long kept his daughter most scrupulously from every human eye, would now let her appear for the first time.

Nathaniel found a card of invitation, and with heart beating high went at the appointed hour to the professor's, where the coaches were already arriving and the lights shining in the decorated rooms. The company was numerous and brilliant. Olympia appeared dressed with great richness and taste. Her beautifully shaped face and her figure roused general admiration. The somewhat strange arch of her back and the wasp-like thinness of her waist seemed to be produced by too tight lacing. In her step and deportment there was something measured and stiff, which struck many as unpleasant, but it was ascribed to the constraint produced by the company. The concert began. Olympia played the harpsichord with great dexterity, and sang a virtuoso piece, with a voice like the sound of a glass bell, clear and almost piercing. Nathaniel was quite enraptured; he stood in the back row, and could not perfectly recognize Olympia's features in the dazzling light. Therefore, quite unnoticed, he took out Coppola's glass and looked towards the fair creature. Ah! then he saw with what a longing glance she gazed towards him, and how every note of her song plainly sprang from that loving glance, whose fire penetrated his inmost soul. Her accomplished roulades seemed to Nathaniel the exultation of a mind transfigured by love, and when at last, after the cadence, the long trill sounded shrilly through the room, he felt as if clutched by burning arms. He could restrain himself no longer, but with mingled pain and rapture shouted out, 'Olympia!'

Everyone looked at him, and many laughed. The organist of the cathedral made a gloomier face than usual, and simply said: 'Well, well.'

The concert had finished, the ball began. 'To dance with her—with her!' That was the aim of all Nathaniel's desire, of all his efforts; but how to gain courage to ask her, the queen of the ball? Nevertheless—he himself did not know how it happened— no sooner had the dancing begun than he was standing close to Olympia, who had not yet been asked to dance. Scarcely able to stammer out a few words, he had seized her hand. Olympia's hand was as cold as ice; he felt a horrible deathly chill thrilling through him. He looked into her eyes, which beamed back full of love and desire, and at the same time it seemed as though her pulse began to beat and her life's blood to flow into her cold hand. And in the soul of Nathaniel the joy of love rose still higher; he clasped the beautiful Olympia, and with her flew through the dance. He thought that his dancing was usually correct as to time, but the peculiarly steady rhythm with which Olympia moved, and which often put him completely out, soon showed him that his time was most defective. However, he would dance with no other lady, and would have murdered anyone who approached Olympia for the purpose of asking her. But this only happened twice, and to his astonishment Olympia remained seated until the next dance, when he lost no time in making her rise again.

Had he been able to see any other object besides the fair Olympia, all sorts of unfortunate quarrels would have been inevitable. For the quiet, scarcely suppressed laughter which arose among the young people in every corner was manifestly directed towards Olympia, whom they followed with very curious glances—one could not tell why. Heated by the dance and by the wine, of which he had freely partaken, Nathaniel had laid aside all his ordinary reserve. He sat by Olympia with her hand in his and, in a high state of inspiration, told her his passion, in words which neither he nor Olympia understood.

Yet perhaps she did; for she looked steadfastly into his face and sighed several times, 'Ah, ah!' Upon this, Nathaniel said, 'Oh splendid, heavenly lady! Ray from the promised land of love— deep soul in whom all my being is reflected !' with much more stuff of the like kind. But Olympia merely went on sighing, 'Ah—ah!'

Professor Spalanzani occasionally passed the happy pair, and smiled on them with a look of singular satisfaction. To Nathaniel, although he felt in quite another world, it seemed suddenly as though Professor Spalanzani's face was growing considerably darker, and when he looked around he perceived, to his no small horror, that the last two candles in the empty room had burned down to their sockets, and were just going out. The music and dancing had ceased long ago.

'Parting—parting!' he cried in wild despair; he kissed Olympia's hand, he bent towards her mouth, when his glowing lips were met by lips cold as ice! Just as when he had touched her cold hand, he felt himself overcome by horror; the legend of the dead bride darted suddenly through his mind, but Olympia pressed him fast, and her lips seemed to spring to life at his kiss. Professor Spalanzani strode through the empty hall, his steps caused a hollow echo, and his figure, round which a flickering shadow played, had a fearful, spectral appearance.

'Do you love me, do you love me, Olympia? Only one word! Do you love me?' whispered Nathaniel; but as she rose Olympia only sighed, 'Ah—ah!'

'Yes, my gracious, my beautiful star of love,' said Nathaniel, 'you have risen upon me, and you will shine, for ever lighting my inmost soul.'

'Ah—ah!' replied Olympia, as she departed. Nathaniel followed her; they both stood before the professor.

'You have had a very animated conversation with my daughter,' said he, smiling; 'So, dear Herr Nathaniel, if you have any pleasure in talking with a silly girl, your visits shall be welcome.'

Nathaniel departed with a whole heaven beaming in his heart. The next day Spalanzani's party was the general subject of conversation. Notwithstanding that the professor had made every effort to appear splendid, the wags had all sorts of incongruities and oddities to talk about. They were particularly hard upon the dumb, stiff Olympia whom, in spite of her beautiful exterior, they considered to be completely stupid, and they were delighted to find in her stupidity the reason why Spalanzani had kept her so long concealed. Nathaniel did not hear this without secret anger. Nevertheless he held his peace. 'For,' thought he, 'is it worth while convincing these fellows that it is their own stupidity that prevents their recognizing Olympia's deep, noble mind?'

One day Sigismund said to him: 'Be kind enough, brother, to tell me how a sensible fellow like you could possibly lose your head over that wax face, over that wooden doll up there?'

Nathaniel was about to fly out in a passion, but he quickly recollected himself and retorted: 'Tell me, Sigismund, how it is that Olympia's heavenly charms could escape your active and intelligent eyes, which generally perceive things so clearly? But, for that very reason, Heaven be thanked, I have not you for my rival; otherwise, one of us must have fallen a bleeding corpse!'

Sigismund plainly perceived his friend's condition. So he skillfully gave the conversation a turn and, after observing that in love-affairs there was no disputing about the object, added:

'Nevertheless, it is strange that many of us think much the same about Olympia. To us—pray do not take it ill, brother she appears singularly stiff and soulless. Her shape is well proportioned—so is her face—that is true! She might pass for beautiful if her glance were not so utterly without a ray of life—without the power of vision. Her pace is strangely regular, every movement seems to depend on some wound-up clockwork. Her playing and her singing keep the same unpleasantly correct and spiritless time as a musical box, and the same may be said of her dancing. We find your Olympia quite uncanny, and prefer to have nothing to do with her. She seems to act like a living being, and yet has some strange peculiarity of her own.'

Nathaniel did not completely yield to the bitter feeling which these words of Sigismund's roused in him, but mastered his indignation, and merely said with great earnestness, 'Olympia may appear uncanny to you, cold, prosaic man. Only the poetical mind is sensitive to its like in others. To me alone was the love in her glances revealed, and it has pierced my mind and all my thought; only in the love of Olympia do I discover my real self. It may not suit you that she does not indulge in idle chit-chat like other shallow minds. She utters few words, it is true, but these few words appear as genuine hieroglyphics of the inner world, full of love and deep knowledge of the spiritual life, and contemplation of the eternal beyond. But you have no sense for all this, and my words are wasted on you.'

'God preserve you, brother,' said Sigismund very mildly almost sorrowfully. 'But you seem to me to be in an evil way. You may depend upon me, if all—no, no, I will not say anything further.'

All of a sudden it struck Nathaniel that the cold, prosaic Sigismund meant very well towards him; he therefore shook his proffered hand very heartily.

Nathaniel had totally forgotten the very existence of Clara, whom he had once loved; his mother, Lothaire—all had vanished from his memory; he lived only for Olympia, with whom he sat for hours every day, uttering strange fantastical stuff about his love, about the sympathy that glowed to life, about the affinity of souls, to all of which Olympia listened with great devotion. From the very bottom of his desk he drew out all that he had ever written. Poems, fantasies, visions, romances, tales—this stock was daily increased by all sorts of extravagant sonnets, stanzas and canzoni, and he read them all tirelessly to Olympia for hours on end. Never had he known such an admirable listener. She neither embroidered nor knitted, she never looked out of the window, she fed no favorite bird, she played neither with lapdog nor pet cat, she did not twist a slip of paper or anything else in her hand, she was not obliged to suppress a yawn by a gentle forced cough. In short, she sat for hours, looking straight into her lover's eyes, without stirring, and her glance became more and more lively and animated Only when Nathaniel rose at last, and kissed her hand and her lips did she say, 'Ah, ah!' to which she added: 'Good night, dearest.'

'Oh deep, noble mind!' cried Nathaniel in his own room, 'you, you alone, dear one, fully understand me.'

He trembled with inward rapture, when he considered the wonderful harmony that was revealed more and more every day between his own mind and that of Olympia. For it seemed to him as if Olympia had spoken concerning him and his poetical talent out of the depths of his own mind; as if her voice had actually sounded from within himself. That must indeed have been the case, for Olympia never uttered any words whatever beyond those which have already been recorded. Even when Nathaniel, in clear and sober moments, as for instance upon waking in the morning, remembered Olympia's utter passivity and her painful lack of words, he merely said: 'Words words! The glance of her heavenly eye speaks more than any language here below. Can a child of heaven adapt herself to the narrow confines drawn by a miserable mundane necessity?'

Professor Spalanzani appeared highly delighted at the intimacy between his daughter and Nathaniel. To the latter he gave the most unequivocal signs of approbation; and when Nathaniel ventured at last to hint at a union with Olympia, his whole face smiled as he observed that he would leave his daughter a free choice in the matter. Encouraged by these words and with burning passion in his heart, Nathaniel resolved to implore Olympia on the very next day to say directly and in plain words what her kind glance had told him long ago; namely, that she loved him. He sought the ring which his mother had given him at parting, to give it to Olympia as a symbol of his devotion, of his life which budded forth and bloomed with her alone. Clara's letters and Lothaire's came to his hands during the search; but he flung them aside indifferently, found the ring, pocketed it and hastened over to Olympia. Already on the steps, in the hall, he heard a strange noise, which seemed to proceed from Spalanzani's room. There was a stamping, a clattering, a pushing, a banging against the door, intermingled with curses and imprecations.

Let go—let go! Rascal!—Scoundrel!—Body and soul I've risked upon it!—Ha, ha, ha!—That's not what we agreed to!—I, I made the eyes!—I made the clockwork!—Stupid blockhead with your clockwork!—Accursed dog of a bungling watchmaker!—OR with you!—Devil!—Stop !—Pipe-maker!—Infernal beast!—Stop !—Get out!—Let go!'

These words were uttered by the voices of Spalanzani and the hideous Coppelius, who were raging and wrangling together. Nathaniel rushed in, overcome by the most inexpressible anguish.

The professor was holding a female figure fast by the shoulders, the Italian Coppola grasped it by the feet, and there they were tugging and pulling, this way and that, contending for the possession of it with the utmost fury. Nathaniel started back with horror when in the figure he recognized Olympia. Boiling with the wildest indignation, he was about to rescue his beloved from these infuriated men. But at that moment Coppola, whirling round with the strength of a giant, wrenched the figure from the professor's hand, and then dealt him a tremendous blow with the object itself, which sent him reeling and tumbling backwards over the table, upon which stood vials, retorts, bottles and glass cylinders. All these were dashed to a thousand shivers. Now Coppola flung the figure across his shoulders, and with a frightful burst of shrill laughter dashed down the stairs, so fast that the feet of the figure, which dangled in the most hideous manner, rattled with a wooden sound on every step.

Nathaniel stood paralyzed; he had seen but too plainly that Olympia's waxen, deathly-pale countenance had no eyes, but black holes instead—she was, indeed, a lifeless doll. Spalanzani was writhing on the floor; the pieces of glass had cut his head, his breast and his arms, and the blood was spurting up as from so many fountains. But he soon collected all his strength.

'After him—after him—what are you waiting for ? Coppelius, Coppelius—has robbed me of my best automaton—a work of twenty years—body and soul risked upon it—the clockwork—the speech—the walk, mine; the eyes stolen from you. The infernal rascal—after him; fetch Olympia—there you see the eyes!'

And now Nathaniel saw that a pair of eyes lay upon the ground, staring at him; these Spalanzani caught up, with his unwounded hand, and flung into his bosom. Then madness seized Nathaniel in its burning claws, and clutched his very soul, destroying his every sense and thought.

'Ho—ho—ho—a circle of fire! of fire! Spin round, circle! Merrily, merrily! Ho, wooden doll—spin round, pretty doll!' he cried, flying at the professor, and clutching at his throat.

He would have strangled him had not the noise attracted a crowd, who rushed in and forced Nathaniel to let go, thus saving the professor, whose wounds were immediately dressed. Sigismund, strong as he was, was not able to master the mad Nathaniel, who kept crying out in a frightening voice: 'Spin round, wooden doll!' and laid about him with clenched fists. At last the combined force of many succeeded in overcoming him, in flinging him to the ground and binding him. His words were merged into one hideous roar like that of a brute, and in this insane condition he was taken raging to the mad-house.

Before I proceed to tell you, gentle reader, what more befell the unfortunate Nathaniel, should you by chance take an interest in that skilful optician and automaton-maker Spalanzani, I can inform you that he was completely healed of his wounds. He was, however, obliged to leave the university, because Nathaniel's story had created a sensation, and it was universally considered a quite unpardonable trick to smuggle a wooden doll into respectable tea-parties in place of a living person—for Olympia had been quite a success at tea-parties. The lawyers called it a most subtle deception, and the more culpable, inasmuch as he had planned it so artfully against the public that not a single soul—a few cunning students excepted—had detected it, although all now wished to play the wiseacre, and referred to various facts which had appeared to them suspicious. Nothing very clever was revealed in this way. Would it strike anyone as so very suspicious, for instance, that, according to the expression of an elegant tea-ite, Olympia had, contrary to all usage, sneezed oftener than she had yawned ? 'The former,' remarked this fashionable person, 'was the sound of the concealed clockwork winding itself up. Moreover, it had creaked audibly.' And so on.

The professor of poetry and eloquence took a pinch of snuff, clapped the lid of his box to, cleared his throat, and said solemnly: 'Ladies and gentlemen, do you not perceive where the trick lies? It is all an allegory—a sustained metaphor—you understand me—sapient! sat.

But many were not satisfied with this; the story of the automaton had struck deep root into their souls and, in fact, a pernicious mistrust of human figures in general had begun to creep in. Many lovers, to be quite convinced that they were not enamoured of wooden dolls, would request their mistresses to sing and dance a little out of time, to embroider and knit, and play with their lapdogs, while listening to reading, etc., and, above all, not merely to listen, but also sometimes to talk, in such a manner as presupposed actual thought and feeling. With many the bond of love became firmer and more entrancing, though others, on the contrary, slipped gently out of the noose. One cannot really answer for this,' said some. At tea parties yawning prevailed to an incredible extent, and there was no sneezing at all, that all suspicion might be avoided. Spalanzani, as already stated, was obliged to decamp, to escape a criminal prosecution for fraudulently introducing an automaton into human society. Coppola had vanished also.

Nathaniel awakened as from a heavy, frightful dream; as he opened his eyes, he felt an indescribable sensation of pleasure glowing through him with heavenly warmth. He was in bed in his own room, in his father s house, Clara was stooping over him, and Lothaire and his mother were standing near.

'At last, at last, beloved Nathaniel, you have recovered from your serious illness—now you are mine again!' said Clara, from the very depth of her soul, and clasped Nathaniel in her arms.

It was with mingled sorrow and delight that the bright tears fell from his eyes, as he answered with a deep sigh: 'My own—my own Clara!'

Sigismund, who had faithfully remained with his friend in his hour of trouble, now entered. Nathaniel stretched out his hand to him. 'And you, faithful brother, have you not deserted me?'

Every trace of Nathaniel's madness had vanished, and he soon gained strength under the care of his mother, his beloved and his friends. Good fortune also had visited the house, for a miserly old uncle of whom nothing had been expected had died, leaving their mother, besides considerable property, an estate in a pleasant spot near the town. Thither Nathaniel decided to go, with his Clara, whom he now intended to marry, his mother and Lothaire. He had grown milder and more docile than ever he had been before, and now, for the first time, he understood the heavenly purity and the greatness of Clara's mind. No one, by the slightest hint, reminded him of the past.

Only, when Sigismund took leave of him, Nathaniel said: 'Heavens, brother, I was in an evil way, but a good angel led me betimes on to the path of light! Ah, that was Clara!'

Sigismund did not let him carry the discourse further for fear that grievous recollections might burst forth in all their lurid brightness.

At about this time the four lucky persons thought of going to the estate. It was noon and they were walking in the streets of the city, where they had made several purchases. The high steeple of the townhall was already casting its gigantic shadow over the market-place.

'Oh,' said Clara, 'let us climb it once more and look out at the distant mountains!'

No sooner said than done. Nathaniel and Clara both ascended the steps, the mother returned home with the servant, and Lothaire, who was not inclined to clamber up so many stairs, chose to remain below. The two lovers stood arm-in-arm on the highest gallery of the tower, and looked down upon the misty forests, behind which the blue mountains rose like a gigantic city.

'Look there at that curious little grey bush,' said Clara. 'It actually looks as if it were striding towards us.'

Nathaniel mechanically put his hand into his breast pocket—he found Coppola's telescope, and pointed it to one side. Clara was in the way of the glass. His pulse and veins leapt convulsively. Pale as death, he stared at Clara, soon streams of fire flashed and glared from his rolling eyes, he roared frightfully, like a hunted beast.Then he sprang high into the air and. punctuating his words with horrible laughter, he shrieked out in a piercing tone, 'Spin round, wooden doll!—spin round!' Then seizing Clara with immense force, he tried to hurl her down, but with the desperate strength of one battling against death she clutched the railings.

Lothaire heard the' raging of the madman—he heard Clara's shriek of agony—fearful forebodings darted through his mind, he ran up, the door to the second flight was fastened, Clara's shrieks became louder and still louder. Frantic with rage and anxiety, he threw himself against the door, which finally burst open. Clara's voice was becoming weaker and weaker. 'Help—help save me!' With these words the voice seemed to die on the air.

'She is gone—murdered by that madman!' cried Lothaire.

The door of the gallery was also closed, but despair gave him a giant's strength, and he burst it from the hinges. Heavens! Grasped by the mad Nathaniel, Clara was hanging in the air over the gallery—with one hand only she still held one of the iron railings. Quick as lightning, Lothaire caught his sister and drew her in, at the same moment striking the madman in the face with his clenched fist to such effect that he reeled and let go his prey.

Lothaire ran down with his fainting sister in his arms. She was saved. Nathaniel went raging about the gallery, leaping high in the air and crying, 'Circle of fire'spin round! spin round!'

The people collected at the sound of his wild shrieks and among them, prominent for his gigantic stature, was the advocate Coppelius, who had just come to the town, and was proceeding straight to the market-place. Some wished to climb up and secure the madman, but Coppelius only laughed, saying, 'Ha, ha—just wait—he will soon come down of his own accord,' and looked up like the rest Nathaniel suddenly stood still as if petrified.

Then, perceiving Coppelius, he stooped down, and yelled out, 'Ah, pretty eyes—pretty eyes!' with which he sprang over the railing.

When Nathaniel lay on the stone pavement with his head shattered, Coppelius had disappeared in the crowd.

Many years afterwards it is said that Clara was seen in a remote spot, sitting hand in hand with a kind-looking man before the door of a country house, while two lively boys played before her. From this it may be inferred that she at last found a quiet domestic happiness suitable to her serene and cheerful nature, a happiness which the morbid Nathaniel would never have given her.